Rock-a-bye Baby

You rock!

Rock-a-bye Baby

Danny Adlerman
Illustrated by **Kim Adlerman**

 Charlesbridge

The artist would like to thank her mother, Lillian, for allowing her to use the personally crocheted afghan, and her children: Rachelle, for having and donating such beautiful hair; Josh, for being so cool; and Maxx, for being a model boy. . . or more accurately, boy model. I love you.

To illustrate this book, the artist first painted a watercolor base plate. She then applied varying layers of painted figures in conjunction with leaves, dried flowers, stones, cross-stitch, and other fabrics, feathers, clay models, pencil shavings, her daughter's hair, crocheted afghan, and lots of glue. The world is art.

Published by Charlesbridge
85 Main Street
Watertown, MA 02472
(617) 926-0329
www.charlesbridge.com

Library of Congress Cataloging-in-Publication Data
Adlerman, Daniel, 1963-
   Rock-a-bye baby / Danny Adlerman ; illustrated by Kim Adlerman.
   p. cm.
Summary: An extended version of the familiar lullaby that takes baby
through hills and valleys until he finds sleep in his mother's arms.
   ISBN 1-58089-082-2 (reinforced for library use)
   1. Children's songs—Texts. 2. Lullabies. [1. Songs. 2. Lullabies.]
I. Adlerman, Kimberly M., 1964- ill. II. Title.
   PZ8.3.A2329Ro 2004
   782.42—dc21   2003003735

Printed in China
(hc) 10 9 8 7 6 5 4 3 2 1

Display and text type set in Tiffany
Transparencies of artwork collages by
   Gamma One Conversions, Inc.
Color separated, printed, and bound
   by P. Chan & Edward, Inc.
Production supervision by Danny Adlerman

For Rachelle,
Beautiful. Intelligent. Sensitive. Independent.
And best of all, my daughter. I love you.
        —Daddy

For Mom, who blankets me with love,
and for Dad, who shows me the way
        —K. A.

Rock-a-bye baby on the treetop,
When the wind blows, the cradle will rock.

When the bough breaks, the cradle will fall,
And down will come baby, cradle and all.

Down slides the cradle, baby inside,
Snuggled in blankets, gently does glide.
When the rains come, he slips in the stream,
And soon the sweet baby, sleepy, will dream.

Cradle and baby sail down the creek,
Blanket caressing softly his cheek.
Dreaming of clouds in the sky above,
He's feeling warm,
    and he's feeling loved.

Soon the young child awakes from his nap,
Happily sees a friend in his lap.
Baby and playmate gently will play;
Breeze will entice the friends both away.

As the wind gusts through valley and hill,
Baby and cradle and bear all are still.
Through the pass slowly they start their ride,
Path close and narrow, eyes open wide.

Soon at the bottom, next to the green,
Child at peace, his world is serene.
A passing traveler lands on his toes;
Baby is curious, butterfly knows.

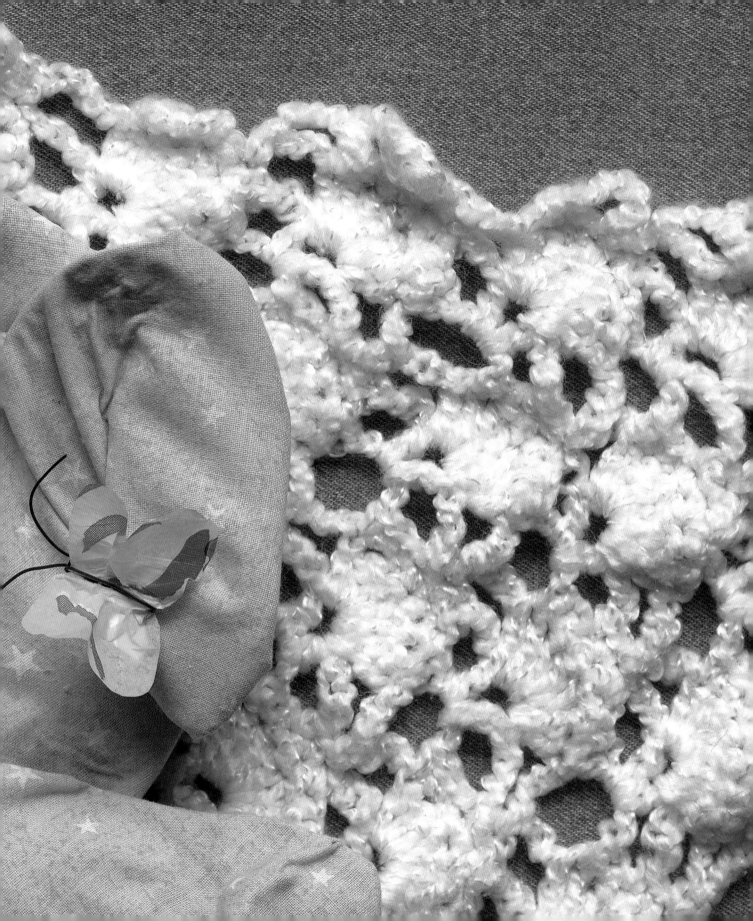

Wind blowing slowly, rustling the trees,
Leaves swirling gently tickle his knees.

Birds singing sweetly, gracefully play
Soon to transport the child away.

Tops of the mountains, covered with snow,
Lazily floating over they go.

Lifted to safety, close to the sky,
Blanket and Teddy, both warm and dry.

Resting the cradle, child inside
Lovingly smiles thanks for the ride.
Hillside is wondrous, humble but bold;
Baby so young, and mountain so old.

Over the meadow, sunset will creep,
Soon it is time for baby to sleep.
A perfect ending, a perfect day,
As mother carries baby away.

Rock-a-bye Baby

Rock-a-bye ba-by on the tree-top,

When the wind blows, the cra-dle will rock.

When the bough breaks, the cra-dle will fall, And

down will come ba-by, cra-dle and all.

1. Rock-a-bye baby on the treetop,
When the wind blows, the cradle will rock.
When the bough breaks, the cradle will fall,
And down will come baby, cradle and all.

2. Down slides the cradle, baby inside,
Snuggled in blankets, gently does glide.
When the rains come, he slips in the stream,
And soon the sweet baby, sleepy, will dream.

3. Cradle and baby sail down the creek,
Blanket caressing softly his cheek.
Dreaming of clouds in the sky above,
He's feeling warm, and he's feeling loved.

4. Soon the young child awakes from his nap,
Happily sees a friend in his lap.
Baby and playmate gently will play;
Breeze will entice the friends both away.

5. As the wind gusts through valley and hill,
Baby and cradle and bear all are still.
Through the pass slowly they start their ride,
Path close and narrow, eyes open wide.

6. Soon at the bottom, next to the green,
Child at peace, his world is serene.
A passing traveler lands on his toes;
Baby is curious, butterfly knows.

7. Wind blowing slowly, rustling the trees,
Leaves swirling gently tickle his knees.
Birds singing sweetly, gracefully play
Soon to transport the child away.

8. Tops of the mountains, covered with snow,
Lazily floating over they go.
Lifted to safety, close to the sky,
Blanket and Teddy, both warm and dry.

9. Resting the cradle, child inside
Lovingly smiles thanks for the ride.
Hillside is wondrous, humble but bold;
Baby so young, and mountain so old.

10. Over the meadow, sunset will creep,
Soon it is time for baby to sleep.
A perfect ending, a perfect day,
As mother carries baby away.